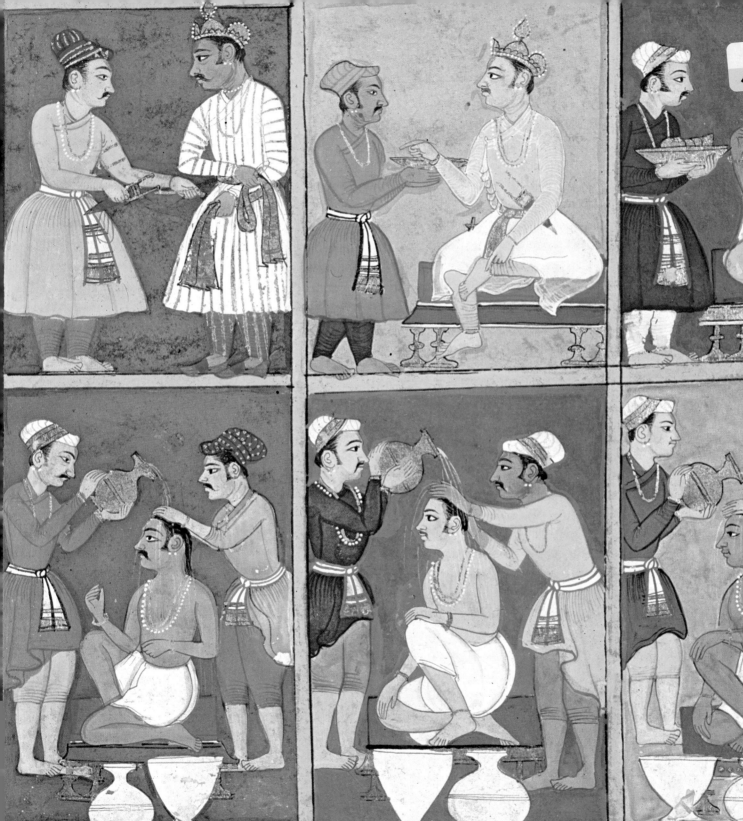
KT-545-704

The Story of
Prince Rama

Brian Thompson

The Story of Prince Rama

Illustrated by original paintings
and by Jeroo Roy

Kestrel Books

For Sheila Burke

KESTREL BOOKS
Published by Penguin Books Ltd
Harmondsworth, Middlesex, England

Copyright © by Brian Thompson 1980

Illustrations Copyright © by Jeroo Roy 1980

All rights reserved. No part of this publication may be
reproduced, stored in a retrieval system, or transmitted
in any form or by any means, electronic, mechanical,
photocopying, recording, or otherwise, without the prior
permission of the Copyright owner.

First published in 1980

ISBN 0 7226 5684 X

Typeset in Great Britain by
Western Printing Services Ltd, Bristol

Printed in Great Britain by
Sackville Press (Billericay) Ltd, Billericay, Essex.

Acknowledgements

The author and publishers would like to thank the
following for their kind permission to reproduce
illustrative material:

The British Library for the jacket illustrations, endpapers
and pp. 7, 9, 11, 13, 15, 17, 19, 21, 23, 25, 27, 29, 51, 53,
55, 57, 59, 61, 63; Cleveland Museum of Art, Cleveland,
Ohio for p. 45; the Director of the India Office Library and
Records for pp. 43, 47; Sotheby Parke Bernet Publications
for p. 41; Victoria and Albert Museum for pp. 1, 2.

Jeroo Roy's illustrations appear on pp. 31, 33, 35, 37, 39, 49.

A note about the pictures

The Indian paintings in this book are over three hundred years old. Many of them come from Udaipur in western India where they were painted to illustrate a manuscript of the Ramayana story for the king of Udaipur, Jagat Singh. Most of this manuscript is now in the British Library in London. It has about four hundred paintings in all. The Kings of Udaipur were the chiefs of all the Hindu princes of India, and were said to be descended from Rama himself.

These paintings, which are called Rajput paintings after the Rajput kings who had them made, are mostly in hot bright colours, without much shading. You must imagine them being examined in the gloom of royal palaces, shielded from the hot glare of the sun outside by great stone walls and by coverings on the small windows. As the royal women often could not read the text of the manuscript, the pictures had to be very detailed, each picture telling a whole sequence of events. This is the reason why the same people sometimes appear two or more times in the same picture.

Rama is usually painted dark blue in colour. He is thought of as the god Vishnu, whom Hindus always call dark, in contrast to the other great god, Shiva, who is white.

Guide to pronunciation

There are various types of sounds in Indian languages which do not occur in English, but here is a rough guide for pronouncing the names in the story.

The vowel 'a' is difficult: sometimes it is short and is pronounced 'uh' like the 'u' in 'rut' – not like the 'a' in 'rat'; sometimes the 'a' is pronounced 'ah' as in 'Ma'. In the guide the names are split up into syllables, or sounds, to show how they should be said; try not to stress one syllable more than another, but give them equal weight.

Name	Approximate pronunciation
Bharata	Buh-rat-uh
Dasharatha	Dash-uh-rat-uh
Hanuman	Han-u-mahn
Janaka	Jan-uh-kuh
Kaikeyi	Ky-kay-ee
Lakshmana	Luksh-man-uh
Rama	Rah-mah
Ravana	Rah-van-uh
Shatrughna	Shuh-tru-g-nuh
Sita	See-tah

J. P. Losty
Department of Oriental Manuscripts and Books
The British Library

5

The Birth of Prince Rama

Good King Dasharatha had three wives but no children. He lived in a beautiful palace and the land that he ruled was peaceful and rich. The farms and the orchards grew more than enough food for all the people. The rivers were busy with boats loaded down with precious goods. Even the weather in the kingdom was specially kind and the seasons followed one another sweetly, year in and year out. Everyone in the land was happy and contented. Everyone, that is, except King Dasharatha. The king was unhappy because above all else he wanted to have a son to rule the land after him.

King Dasharatha went to see the wisest man in the whole country and asked him what he should do to have a son. The wise man thought for a while and then he told the king that he should pray to the gods and make special sacrifices to please them. If the gods were pleased with the king they would tell him what to do.

The king did as he was told. He prayed and he prayed. He built a huge bonfire and he made the sacrifices. Suddenly, right in the middle of the fire, a god appeared. King Dasharatha moved closer and he saw that the god was carrying a golden bowl. The god spoke. "In this bowl there is a magic mixture of rice and milk. You must share this between your wives and they will all have great sons."

King Dasharatha gave the magic food to his wives and, in time, each of the three wives had sons. They called the sons Rama and Bharata, and the wife who had twin boys called them Lakshmana and Shatrugnha.

The Boyhood of Rama

Rama grew into a strong and handsome boy. King Dasharatha loved each of his four sons but he had a special place in his heart for Rama.

The king wanted his sons to grow up to be wise rulers so he brought the best teachers in the land to the palace. The four boys were taught by the wisest of men.

Rama and his brother Lakshmana became the closest of friends. At the same time the other two brothers, Bharata and Shatrughna, also became fast friends.

Rama learned the skills and arts that a young prince needed. He learned how to ride horses and elephants. He learned how to drive a chariot and how to use the weapons of war.

When Rama was fifteen years old his teacher decided that he had learned how to use the strength of his body and that he should go on to learn to use the power of his soul.

9

Rama and the Terrible She-Monster

Not far from the land of King Dasharatha lived a terrible she-monster. She hated every single living thing on earth and she killed all the animals and birds that came near her. She also killed the trees and flowers and grass and made the countryside around her home a desert. Everyone feared her and no-one would go near the place where she lived.

Rama's teacher explained to Rama that he and Lakshmana were going to have to kill this terrible creature. He said that they could take only bows and arrows and that they would need all the courage they could find in their hearts. So the two princes set out with their teacher.

Soon they left King Dasharatha's beautiful land and journeyed to the place where the she-monster lived. All around the ground was burned and bare.

As soon as the terrible she-monster saw them coming she leaped up into the air and hurled a huge three-pronged spear straight at Rama. Quick as a flash Rama strung an arrow and fired it at the spear. He hit the spear in mid-flight and it turned harmlessly aside. The she-monster roared with fury and hurled rocks at Rama, Lakshmana and the teacher. The three of them shot the rocks out of the sky. Rama aimed very carefully and shot the she-monster dead.

Rama and Lakshmana had proved their courage. The gods were pleased with them and they told Rama that they had a very special plan for his life. Rama, they said, would have many adventures and one day he would have to fight Ravana, the King of all the Demons. Rama knew that Ravana would be a terrible enemy. He was strong and cunning and he had ten heads and twenty arms.

11

The Journey

Rama and Lakshmana journeyed with their teacher. They travelled through deserts and forests and many lonely places. Rama and his brother learned about the countryside they travelled through. They had many adventures and saw strange and wonderful things.

In some of the lonely places in India, far from the cities and the busy towns, there live holy men. Rama and Lakshmana were taken to visit many of these wise men. If, as sometimes happened, the holy men were pestered by tormenting demons who tried to keep them from their prayers, the two brothers fought the demons and chased them off, making the lonely places peaceful once more.

So the two brothers travelled far and wide, until one day they came to the land ruled by King Janaka. The king was delighted to see Rama and Lakshmana and he was especially pleased to meet their teacher who was very famous. The three travellers had arrived at King Janaka's city in time for a special feast. The streets were crowded with people. There were stalls selling sweets and fruits. All the people were dressed in their finest clothes. People were dancing and singing in the streets. There were horse races and elephant fights.

13

Princess Sita

The celebrations in the town were being watched by King Janaka's adopted daughter, a beautiful princess called Sita. Like Rama's father, King Janaka had had no children. Years ago he had prayed to the Goddess of the Earth who had taken pity on him and had given him Sita. He had found Sita when she was a little baby, lying in a furrow in a ploughed field.

King Janaka had loved the beautiful baby girl and he brought her up as if she was his very own daughter. Sita was now sitting on a balcony, surrounded by her attendants, watching the festival. As Rama walked along the street among the happy people he looked up at the palace balcony and he saw Sita. He thought she was the most beautiful princess that he had ever seen. Sita noticed Rama in the crowd and she too fell in love at first sight.

Of course many princes had wanted to marry Princess Sita so her father King Janaka had decided that there should be a test to make certain that her husband would be worthy of her.

The king had a magnificent bow that had belonged to one of the great gods of the universe. Once the bow had struck fear into the hearts of some of the most dreadful demons. It was so powerful that no ordinary man could even bend it a little. The bow did not have a bowstring and King Janaka had promised that he would give Sita as a bride to any prince who could bend the bow and notch the string into place. Year after year princes came to try to win Sita for a wife, but not one of them ever bent the bow even slightly.

When King Janaka heard that Rama sought to marry Sita he was delighted. He ordered the bow to be brought to Rama. Rama gripped the bow in his hands, but he staggered under its magical, hidden weight. He gritted his teeth and pulled on the bowstring. The bow bent a little. Then the bow bent a little more and a little more. Rama pulled the top of the bow down far enough to fit the bowstring but before he could notch it into place there was an earth-shaking bang and the bow broke in half. Rama had passed the test. He had won Sita for his bride.

15

The Wedding

The King was so pleased that Rama had won the right to marry Sita that he decided that he would make the wedding the greatest one that there had ever been. He sent messengers all round his kingdom to tell the people, and then he began to make splendid preparations.

The news was sent back to Rama's father, King Dasharatha, and he decided that everyone in his palace would also travel to the wedding of Rama and Sita.

Lakshmana's twin brother Shatrughna, and Bharata the fourth of the brothers, travelled with their father to the wedding. King Janaka remembered that Sita had three beautiful cousins who had reached the age when they wanted to marry, so the three cousins of Sita and the three brothers of Rama arranged to marry at the same time as Rama and Sita.

The wedding feast was indeed splendid, quite the greatest one that there had ever been and the people of the two kingdoms celebrated the four-fold wedding.

After the wedding was over, Rama's teacher told him that Rama had now finished his training. The teacher said that he himself was going to say farewell to the court of King Dasharatha and he would now go and travel into the mountains to find a lonely place where he might spend his last years in prayer and holiness.

Rama is to be the King

King Dasharatha returned to his palace after Rama's wedding to Sita and he thought with pride of his dear son. He knew that he was growing old and getting frail so he made his mind up to stop being the king and to let Rama rule the land in his place.

The king announced his decision to his court and he sent his messengers out to the furthest corners of his kingdom. All the people loved Rama and they knew that he would make an excellent king, so the land was full of joy and celebrations.

Rama was proud that his father loved him so much and thought him wise and strong enough to become the king. Rama hurried to tell the news to his mother.

But that night King Dasharatha had nightmares. He dreamed that his own special star, the one that had shone in the sky on the morning of his birth, suddenly burst into flames and crashed down upon the earth. He dreamed that the whole sky was filled with screams and groanings. He woke up very frightened and he sent for Rama. The king warned Rama that he had had very bad dreams and that he thought Rama would have to be very careful and do all the right services for the gods.

19

Queen Kaikeyi

One of Rama's stepmothers was called Queen Kaikeyi. She was the mother of Bharata. At first she was delighted to hear that Rama was going to be the king, but then evil crept into her heart. She had a servant, an old humpbacked woman who had hated Rama since he was a boy. When he was very little Rama had laughed at the servant and made fun of her. Once he had thrown mudballs at her and she had never forgotten this. Now she had a chance to get ger own back on Rama. She began to poison her mistress's mind against Rama. She whispered to Queen Kaikeyi that when Rama became king he would make his own mother the queen of the land and that Queen Kaikeyi would lose her place in the palace.

"Rama will want his own mother to be the most important lady here," the old servant whispered. "You will be neglected." The humpbacked servant talked and talked to Queen Kaikeyi until she became jealous of Rama and longed for her own son, Bharata, to be the king.

Many, many years earlier Queen Kaikeyi had saved the life of King Dasharatha. He had fallen in battle and she had seen him fall under the wheels of a chariot. Queen Kaikeyi had bravely run out and rescued him. She had saved his life and she had nursed him until he was strong and well again. The king had been very grateful to her and he had promised her two wishes as a reward for what she had done. The queen had never claimed these two wishes but now she decided it was time to remind the king of his promise.

"Do you remember, my Lord, when I saved your life, so long ago?"

"Yes, yes, of course I do my dear. But don't look so cross and crotchety. You must cheer up and be ready to celebrate the great feast we will have when we make Rama the king."

"If you remember the time when I saved your life, do you remember what it was that you promised me?"

"Of course I do, dear Queen Kaikeyi," said King Dasharatha, "I promised you the two wishes of your heart, and I said that you could claim these two wishes at any time at all, even if you took a hundred years to decide what it was that you wanted. I will grant your wishes now if it will stop you looking so miserable."

The Promise

"Well, I have made up my mind what it is that I want," said Queen Kaikeyi. "I do not want Rama to be made king. I want my own son, Bharata, to be the one who takes over your kingdom. That is my first wish. My second wish is that Rama should leave this country altogether. He must go away from our kingdom and live in the wilds for twice times seven years. Then he will not be able to make any trouble for me or for Bharata."

At first the king thought that Queen Kaikeyi was joking. When he realized that she was serious he was deeply shocked. He pleaded with her not to claim the wishes. He begged her not to make him keep his promise and not to send Rama away from the palace. King Dasharatha knew that he was an old man and he feared that if Rama was sent away for a long time he would not live to welcome him home again. The queen would not give in. The king could not go back on his word. "Let Rama live on berries and grass," she said cruelly, "He will have to go away from our kingdom. Furthermore, he can't take all those rich clothes that he wears. He will have to have clothes made out of leaves or bark. That will teach him a lesson."

Rama was out hunting with Lakshmana. He was called back to the palace. Rama was told of the promise and of his banishment. He accepted quite calmly that he would have to leave his home for twice times seven years. He asked only that he be allowed to go and say farewell to his own mother.

Everyone was horrified at the news, but Rama did not complain. His mother wept and grieved, but Rama comforted her and said that it was not too bad because he would enjoy living in the forests, he would be making his beloved brother Bharata the king and, furthermore, he would be obeying the words of his father.

23

Rama is Banished

The decorations for the crowning of King Rama were outside the palace but inside all was gloomy and sad. King Dasharatha was in despair. He had been forced to do the thing he least wanted to do. Queen Kaikeyi insisted on having the promise honoured. The king did all he could to make her change her mind but she would not be moved. When he knew that he must banish his dear son, King Dasharatha wept. "The world cannot live without the sun. No animal can live without breath, and I cannot live without my dear Rama."

When Lakshmana heard the news he was furious. He took his bow and ran out into the streets shouting that he would kill anyone who tried to stop Rama from becoming the king. Rama ran after him and told him that he too must obey their father. Both sons should do as their father bid them. Lakshmana finally agreed with Rama but he begged Rama to allow him to go with Rama into exile, to care for him and to guard him. "You must let me stay beside you," he said. "You will need a friend if you are to stay away from home for such a long time."

When Rama and Lakshmana went home to Sita they discovered her packed and ready to go. "I have sold all our goods," she said. "I am coming with you. My place is by the side of Prince Rama."

"So be it," said Rama. "And may the gods protect us all."

Rama, Sita and Lakshmana went to the palace and said farewell to the king.

Rama Leaves

Outside the palace a huge crowd gathered to say goodbye to Rama and Sita and Lakshmana. The people brought a chariot to carry the three friends to the borders of the kingdom. The faces that had been filled with joy at the thought of Rama being made the king were now full of pain and sadness.

Rama, Sita and Lakshmana got into the chariot. They left the city and drove across the country to the border. It took them a whole day to reach the river that marked the boundary of the kingdom. The crowd from the city had followed the friends. They all slept by the side of the river.

In the morning Rama and Sita and Lakshmana said goodbye to all their faithful friends and they crossed the river into the unknown lands. A crowd watched them cross the stream, land on the opposite bank and make their way up into a bamboo grove.

The news of Rama's departure was taken back to the palace. The king was told of all that had happened. It was too much sadness for him to bear. Even before the tellers had finished their tale, the king died of grief.

27

Bharata Hears the News

Bharata was not at the palace while all this was happening. He was visiting his grandfather. As soon as he came back to the palace, his mother, Queen Kaikeyi, met him and told the whole story of how she had arranged things so Bharata would be the new king. Every word his mother spoke made Bharata angrier and angrier. He raged at her for what she had done. He would have killed her in his anger but he knew that Rama would have never forgiven him for such a wicked deed.

Bharata hurried to see Rama's mother and begged her to forgive the evil things that his mother had done. He shut himself up for a time and he grieved for his dead father, the king.

Bharata thought that he would try to find Rama. Shatrughna, his brother, went with him on the long journey to the border of the kingdom. Together the brothers crossed the river and began to search the forests. Shatrughna climbed a tree and saw in the distance a little hut in the forest. Beside the hut was Rama, Sita and Lakshmana.

The four brothers were together again. Bharata begged Rama to forgive him. "I don't want to be the king. Come back home Rama. You must take over the kingdom as our dear father first wished."

"No, I cannot do that," replied Rama, "I must carry out the last wishes of our dear father. I must do as he bid me and stay in exile for twice seven years." Although Bharata begged Rama to return to the palace Rama would not change his mind. Bharata saw that nothing would make Rama alter his decision so he picked up Rama's sandals and he told Rama that he would take the sandals back to the palace and place them on the throne. That way everyone would understand that Bharata was ruling the land for Rama and that the kingship was saved for Rama's return. Bharata said that he would not live in the palace, he would be faithful to Rama and he would not be crowned king.

29

In the Forest

So Rama and Sita lived together in the forest with the faithful Lakshmana. At first Rama tried to persuade Lakshmana to return to the land of their father, but Lakshmana said that he wanted to look after Rama and Sita more than anything else in the world. Furthermore, Lakshmana had been told by his mother that he must do just that.

The three friends moved deeper and deeper into the forest. Each time they moved, Lakshmana built them a house. He was very clever and he made each house strong and beautiful. Lakshmana made use of whatever he could find in the forest and the houses were made of bamboo and branches, of mud and palm leaves. Lakshmana managed to paint and pattern each house with beautiful designs.

Sita made clothes from the things she found in the forest.

Few people ever came so far away from the cities of men. There were holy men who lived in the secret places of the forests. Some of the holy men lived with a pupil who was learning about the ways of the gods. Sometimes Rama, Sita and Lakshmana encountered these wise men and they would always visit them and talk with them. One of the old wise men of the forest was especially holy. He knew everything that was to happen in the future. He was very pleased when the three friends came to see him because he already knew of the great deeds that Rama would do in the years ahead. He greeted the three of them as if they were his own dear children and they all stayed talking for hours.

A Home

The wise man had told the friends of a secret glade deep in the forest. It sounded like the perfect place for them to live. They set off through the woods, over the hills and across streams until they came to the spot. Beside the clear river there was a flat piece of grassland where they could build their house. The clearing was surrounded by flowering vines and shrubs. Wild deer grazed in the forest and ducks quacked from the water. There were date palms and mango trees and plenty of fruits and berries. Peacocks perched in the trees. It was altogether wonderful.

First of all Lakshmana set about cooking a meal and then he began the building of his most beautiful house. All summer long the three friends lived happily together in their new house. They swam in the river and gathered food from the forest round about.

They made a new friend. Rama's father, King Dasharatha, had known a great eagle. When the eagle had heard of the death of the king he sought out Rama in the forest and promised to stay with the friends and protect them from all harm.

No creatures were afraid of Rama, Sita and Lakshmana. They lived in peace and harmony. Autumn came to their secret home. The nights were chilly and the wild birds cried through the morning mists that covered the river. Frost shrivelled the water lilies and the mighty elephant drew back from the icy coldness of the river water.

Rama was like an uncrowned king of the forest. The only thing that ever troubled their calm was when the peace of the forest was broken by the savage demons who would search the lonely places for holy men to torment. The demons were very cunning and they could change their shape. Rama looked after the holy men. He could always see through the demons' disguises and he chased them away and kept the forest safe and peaceful.

Ravana's Sister

You will remember that Rama had been told that he would grow to be strong and wise and eventually he would have to fight Ravana, the King of all the Demons. Ravana had a sister. She did not have ten heads and twenty arms like her brother, but she was really ugly. She was a giant and her hair was scraggy, her red teeth were pointy, and, because she ate so much, her belly was enormous. That was her natural shape. Like most demons she could change herself to look like anything at all.

Ravana's sister wandered past Rama's secret house. She saw the handsome Rama and thought that he looked like a young lion. "He is obviously a prince," she thought. "I will trick him into becoming my husband." She changed herself into a beautiful young princess.

Rama was amazed to see such a pretty girl deep in the heart of the forest. He spoke to her politely and she replied with sweet words, trying to enchant him. When that didn't seem to be having any effect she started to tell lies about Sita. "Sita is a horrible wife to you, you must send her back to her own land and marry me instead." Of course this made Rama angry and he told Ravana's sister to go away and to leave him in peace. But she would not stop bothering him. "My dear brother is very powerful. He will make you the richest man in the world. He will give you a fine palace to live in and all the demons will be your servants forever." Rama knew now that the pretty princess was really a demon in disguise. He walked back into the house and Ravana's sister ran off into the forest, changing back into her own horrible shape as she ran. She went home to her cave and sat and howled at the moon.

Sita in Danger

That night Ravana's horrible sister made a plan. She would kidnap Sita and then, she thought, Rama would marry her.

She crept up to the little house in the forest and waited. After a long time Sita came out alone. She was going into the forest to pick flowers. Ravana's sister began to follow her, jumping from hiding place to hiding place. Lakshmana, who was always vigilant, suddenly noticed what was happening. He ran as fast as he could to try to get to the horrible creature before it grabbed Sita. Ravana's sister decided it was time to attack. She crouched, ready to jump on Sita and, at the same moment, Lakshmana caught up with her and knocked her over.

Ravana's sister was enraged. She turned and attacked Lakshmana. He was forced into fighting the howling monster. She was very strong and powerful and Lakshmana had a hard fight finally to beat her. In the struggle Lakshmana had sliced off her nose and her ears.

Ravana's sister hurried to her brother's palace to tell him what had happened. She begged him to help her avenge herself on the three in the forest. "It is all the fault of that Sita," she cried. "She is far too beautiful. You must send your demon forces, dear brother, and kill them all."

"Dear sister," roared Ravana, "I will take my army and stamp those three worms into the ground." Secretly Ravana was very interested to hear that there was a beautiful princess living deep in the forest. Ravana had many wives and he thought that he might have the chance to gain another wife and revenge his sister at the same time. He got all his men together. The demon army was huge. Ravana set his greatest Demon Warrior in charge with fourteen Demon Warlords. The whole army set out for the forest. As soon as Rama and Lakshmana saw the army with their forks, swords, battle-axes and spears they took their bows and shot the weapons out of the demons' hands. That was the start of a terrible battle. The battle lasted for seven days and at the end of it Rama and Lakshmana were surrounded by fourteen thousand dead demons. Those few who had survived had fled in fright.

37

The Golden Deer

Ravana, the King of all the Demons, was really disturbed. His army had been beaten by two young princes; but what troubled him even more was the description his sister had given him of Sita. Every one of his ten heads buzzed with wicked thoughts about Princess Sita. He dreamed about her all day and all night and he could find no peace. He could not get rid of his thoughts of Sita. He even stopped the seasons of the year, the hours of the day and the seconds and minutes that make up time itself. But nothing worked. He was haunted by dreams of the beautiful girl in the forest. He knew that he couldn't hope to beat Rama and Lakshmana by using his power alone. He decided to try to trick them by treachery and magic.

The next day Rama, Sita and Lakshmana saw a golden deer come out of the forest. It shone in the sunshine and its body was covered with jewels. Sita thought it was the most wonderful thing she had ever seen. "Dear Sita, you shall have it for a pet," promised Rama. "I will catch it for you." Rama started to trail the deer. The deer led Rama away from the house into the deep forest. Further and further went the deer, and further and further followed Rama. Quite suddenly Rama realized that it was a trap. He drew his bow and shot an arrow at the deer. The deer fell down and to Rama's astonishment, it called out for help in Rama's own voice.

Far, far away, back at the house, Lakshmana and Sita could hear faintly the voice of Rama calling for help. Sita was very worried and Lakshmana was too. Lakshmana suspected that it might be a trick, because he knew that it would take a mighty force to harm Rama. Sita begged Lakshmana to go to see if any harm had come to Rama. Lakshmana was very reluctant to leave Sita alone. Sita could only think that Rama might be in need of help somewhere in the forest. Lakshmana took his bow and went in search of Rama. The moment he left the house, the King of all the Demons, Ravana, who had been watching all the time, put his wicked plan into action. Ravana changed himself into an old beggarman and went to Sita.

Sita is Captured

Sita was surprised when she saw the old man. "Welcome to our house," said Sita. "Travellers do not often come this way. Have you travelled far?"

"My dear child," said Ravana, "I have come all the way from a distant island called Lanka. Lanka is across the sea from India. It is the island where all the demons live."

"That's very sad," said Sita. "A poor old man like you living among all those demons."

"Oh my dear princess," said Ravana, "you mustn't believe the things that people tell you about the demons. People do tell dreadful lies about them. They have always been most kind to me."

"My husband, Prince Rama, has vowed to rid the world of all the demons."

"What!" exclaimed Ravana, beginning to get very angry. "Your husband thinks he can kill all the demons in existence! The wretched little upstart. Do you think one baby rabbit could kill all the fighting elephants in the world? What are you talking about?" By this time Ravana was so angry that he started changing back into his own shape. Sita was terrified when she saw the old man sprout ten heads and twenty arms. She cried out for help, but Ravana decided to act quickly. He seized Sita and dragged her to his hidden chariot.

Only one creature saw Ravana and Sita. This was the eagle who had promised to protect the three friends. His sharp eyes saw Ravana carry the struggling Sita on to the chariot. The eagle flew to the rescue. His wings beat so strongly that they made windstorms. Ravana saw the eagle flying in to the attack and he seized a weapon in each of his twenty hands. The eagle crashed into the chariot. Ravana looked at the sharp beak and the strong talons. In one of his hands he held a magic sword. With two great swings of the sword Ravana cut off both of the eagle's wings. The eagle fell and Ravana swung his sword again and struck him in the throat a cruel blow. Ravana drove his chariot away. He had Sita, and now he was going to his home in Lanka.

The Search for Sita

Lakshmana found Rama in the forest. He was standing beside the deer. Both brothers knew now that they had been tricked. They hurried back to the house but there was no sign of Sita. Rama stood like a statue, he was so full of grief. "Rama, my dear brother, we must be quick and find Sita," said Lakshmana. "It isn't impossible, let us search together." Rama took heart and they began the search. They looked all round the house. They searched the forest round about. At last they found the eagle who managed to stay alive until he had told Rama of what he had seen. They now knew that Sita had been stolen away by Ravana, the King of all the Demons. But they did not know where Ravana might have taken her. Day after day, week after week, the two brothers searched India for Sita.

Rama and Lakshmana came to the land of the monkey-people. There was a war going on in the land of the monkey-people between the two brothers who were kings of the country. Rama and Lakshmana stayed long enough to bring peace again to the wise monkey-people. The cleverest and bravest of the monkeys was a General in the monkey army called Hanuman. Hanuman became the closest friend of the two brothers. Hanuman loved Rama and vowed to serve him always.

Hanuman proved to be a true friend from the very beginning. It was Hanuman who decided that the entire monkey army, together with their friends the bears, would help with the search for Sita. The army searched all of India: every mountain and cave, every valley and hiding place, every forest and every jungle in all of India. They did not find Sita but Hanuman did meet an eagle (he was actually a brother of the eagle Ravana had killed) and the eagle remembered that he had seen the wicked Ravana carry Sita across the sea between India and Lanka.

43

Hanuman on the Island of Lanka

What do you think of a man being able to jump from India to the island of Lanka? No man could possibly do it, but Hanuman, Rama's new friend, could and did. The sea between India and Lanka was so wide that Hanuman couldn't see Lanka from the sea shore. He climbed up to the top of a nearby mountain, summoned up all his strength and jumped towards Lanka. He took off from the mountain top with such power that the rocks were crushed beneath his feet. He flew through the sky like a burning star and landed safely on the island.

Hanuman still had to find the place where Sita was kept. At first he thought that Ravana would keep Sita a prisoner in his palace. Hanuman made his way to Ravana's city and to the palace where the King of all the Demons lived with all his wicked wives. With the speed and silence of a cat Hanuman started his search. He found the luxurious rooms where Ravana's favourite wives lived, but Sita was not there. He searched the part of the palace where Ravana's discarded wives lived, sulking and squabbling, but Sita was not there either. Bravely he managed to search Ravana's own apartment but nowhere could he find even a trace of Sita.

Hanuman could not know that Ravana had sworn that he would make Sita agree to marry him. At first he had tried to bribe her by offering her a palace of her very own and hundreds of servants to look after her, but Sita was true to Rama and would have nothing to do with Ravana. Ravana had grown angrier and angrier with Sita and he had told her that he would kill her if she did not agree to be one of his wives. "I will give you a little time to think the matter over," he had said. "I will set my guard of ugly demon women to look after you. And if you do not change your mind and marry me, I will chop you up into little pieces and cook you for my breakfast." Ravana then imprisoned Sita in the darkest part of the great garden of his palace. Under the thickly growing palms and cocoa trees, hidden among the vines and the dark leaves, Sita was kept prisoner. She was surrounded by the terrible demon women like a timid deer in the middle of a circle of wolves.

Hanuman Finds Sita

Hanuman had searched through the palace. Now he started to search the gardens. He climbed up into the shadowy trees and began the task. It was not long before he saw a crowd of demon women. He carefully moved in closer and, at last, he saw, down through the leaves, Sita herself. Sita was pale and sad. She was sorrowing for her Prince Rama. Hanuman moved closer and closer. Very, very softly, so softly that only Sita could hear, Hanuman began to sing a song in praise of Rama. Sita could hardly believe her ears. Could it be that the demons were now tormenting her with thoughts of Rama? She looked closely at the place the song came from, and she moved nearer. Still the song went on. Sita came close enough to see Hanuman in his hiding place. Hanuman had brought Rama's own ring with him, to prove that he was not a spy. He carefully passed the ring to Sita.

With great joy Sita recognized the ring as the one that Rama always wore. Hanuman told Sita of the adventures that had happened to Rama and Lakshmana as the two brothers had searched all of India for Sita. He told her the story of how Rama and Lakshmana had come to Hanuman's own land and brought peace to the monkey-people. Hanuman told Sita about the army that had searched for her, and of the eagle who had given them the news that she had been taken to Lanka. Sita was full of happiness. She unknotted a corner of her sari and took out a jewel that she had kept hidden there. She gave the jewel to Hanuman but, as she did so, one of the demon women saw what was going on, and pounced. Hanuman was captured, and the demons dragged him off to the palace to Ravana.

Hanuman wasn't frightened. He had fought in many wars and he had seen many terrible things. He knew that Ravana would have to obey the law that said that a messenger must never be killed. He was brought before Ravana.

Hanuman and Ravana

"Ravana," said Hanuman, "I bring you a message from Prince Rama. He says that you must return Sita to him. What is more he wants you to give up your evil ways or he will come to the island of Lanka with an army to destroy you and all your wicked demons. You do remember that you sent the army of the fourteen demon warlords to revenge your sister and Rama and Lakshmana had no trouble dealing with them."

"I would gladly fight Rama and Lakshmana again," roared Ravana. "And I haven't forgotten what they did to my poor dear sister. If I fight them again I will use all my demons. Tell that to Rama! First of all I will show you, you miserable little monkey, what I do to those who work for Rama!" Ravana turned to his men, "I want you to make a fool out of this monkey. I want you to carry him around the city. But first of all bring me a big bundle of rags." The soldiers brought the rags and Ravana tied the bundle to Hanuman's tail. Next he dipped the tail and the rags into a big pot of oil. The demons brought a burning branch and set fire to the oil. Screaming and roaring, the demons carried Hanuman outside the palace. The fire looked frightening but Hanuman found that it didn't burn his tail.

Hanuman was clever as well as brave and he waited for a chance to escape. As soon as they passed under a tree, Hanuman leaped up and climbed right up into the branches. In a moment he was up on the roofs of Ravana's city. Hanuman discovered that the buildings burned much better than his tail did and he leaped about setting the city ablaze. Fires filled the sky above Lanka. Hanuman had done his work well. He dived into the sea and the fire on his tail sizzled out. He was delighted to find that not one hair had been harmed. Hanuman climbed a hill and sprang back to India.

Rama and Lakshmana prepared for war. There was a vast army of monkeys and bears collecting boulders and rocks; they used everything from stones to the tops of mountains to build the great bridge they would need to cross to Ravana's kingdom.

Before the War

On the island of Lanka Ravana called a council of war. The generals were worried. Outside the palace the great city was still burning and smoking. Many of the demons had lost friends or relations in the fire and, what made them angriest of all, Hanuman had escaped and rejoined Rama and Lakshmana. The Demon Warriors and Demon Warlords planned their attack on Rama's army.

"Our army will easily beat the monkeys and the bears," said Ravana, "but I want to kill Rama and Lakshmana myself. We will have to plan many tricks to try to frighten them. We can protect ourselves with magic fire and we can use our magic invisible arrows that turn into poisonous snakes when they hit their targets."

While the council of war went on, the news was brought to Ravana that the monkeys and bears had com-pleted building the huge bridge across the sea from India and their army was matching across it to Lanka.

Two of Ravana's spies rushed into the council chamber. They had been sent to spy on Rama and Lakshmana but they had been captured. They told Ravana the story of how they had been brought before the two brothers. The spies had expected to be killed, but Rama had been merciful. "Mighty Ravana," they said, "Rama said that we were not to be killed. He showed us all his army. He said that if we came back and told you how very powerful the monkeys and the bears were, and how great their army was, that you would stop the war, free Sita and everyone would live in peace." This news made Ravana even angrier. He gave orders for the battle to begin. The gates of the city opened and Ravana's army poured out. The soldiers spread across the plain like a wall of fire.

51

The War Begins

Rama and Lakshmana watched Ravana's army approach. While Ravana had been holding his council of war they had surrounded the city. The battle started.

The monkeys were fearless fighters. They fought with huge rocks and even trees that they pulled up out of the ground. In close combat they used their fists and claws and teeth. The first battle was terrible to see.

The demon army fought with weapons, but they used trickery whenever they could. They had made a dummy which looked exactly like Sita, and they carried this into the middle of the field of battle and pretended to kill it. The monkeys saw it happen and thought that Princess Sita had been murdered. They were so sad at the thought of this that they all wept, and Ravana's soldiers attacked them savagely. One of the monkey commanders suddenly noticed that the figure was a dummy and not really Sita. The news spread rapidly among the monkey army and they were all so angry that they attacked more fiercely.

One of Ravana's demon brothers flew up into the clouds with the magic invisible snake-arrows. Hidden among the clouds he fired the poisonous arrows at Rama and Lakshmana. They were terrible weapons. Each arrow flew straight to its target and then turned into the deadliest snakes in the world. The two brothers were covered with the snakes. They could not see where the snake-arrows came from. Again and again they were bitten by the snakes and they both fell down dying. Ravana heard this news and sent Sita in a flying chariot over the battlefield cruelly to make her see Rama and Lakshmana lying almost dead. It was a terrible moment for Sita. But the brothers were saved by one of the eagles. A huge eagle flew low over them both. Now all snakes are terrified of eagles, even magic snakes. So, as soon as the eagle appeared, the snakes fled. The poison didn't work if the snake-arrows weren't nearby, so the two brothers recovered immediately.

The Magic Herbs

That day was the first of many days and nights of fighting. There are thousands of tales to be told of the battles and the bravery of the war against Ravana. Ravana used all the trickery he knew; he even wakened the terrible giant-of-all-the-giants from his half-year sleep and sent him into the battle but, in spite of all his treachery Ravana saw that he was losing the war. It was time to send in his own son, who was a Prince and a Demon Warlord.

First of all Ravana made his son completely invisible. He gave him powerful invisible weapons to take into battle. Lastly Ravana surrounded his son with a spell that made a wall of invisible fire around him that would protect him from any stray arrows. So Ravana's son stormed out into the middle of the monkeys and the bears. He killed everyone about him. It was a terrible time for Rama and Lakshmana. No-one could see where the deadly arrows came from. No-one could stop the killing. Everyone fought bravely but they could not see the enemy. The whole army soon lay dead or dying. Lakshmana and Rama ran everywhere trying to find the demon but at last they too were struck down. It was the worst moment of the whole war.

Hanuman was the only soldier still unharmed. He was full of grief and anger. Close by him he saw one of the wisest and oldest of the bears who beckoned desperately to Hanuman. "There is a cure that will work against this terrible weapon," said the dying bear. "You must go to the Himalaya Mountains and seek out four of the special herbs that grow there. They will cancel out the effect of these invisible arrows. If you can do it quickly they will even bring the dead soldiers to life again." Hanuman wasted no time at all. He crossed back to India and to the mountains. There was no time to find the special herbs. He simply lifted the top off a mountain and flew back to Lanka with it. As soon as the mountain-top came near the battlefield the herbs began their work. In no time at all the army was restored to life and health. Hanuman was so thrilled that he lifted Lakshmana up on his own shoulders. Lakshmana could now see Ravana's son and, still sitting on Hanuman's shoulders, he reached over the top of the wall of invisible fire and cut off the demon's head.

Rama and Ravana

Ravana could see that Rama's army was winning the war. There was only one thing left for him to do. He would have to fight Rama himself. He would need all his evil powers in the battle. Ravana prepared himself. He put on his special armour to protect every one of his ten heads and twenty arms. He called for his chariot and rode out to battle.

The gods knew that Rama would need their support in the battle. They gave Rama a chariot. It was a special chariot that could carry over the seas and the mountains.

And so Rama and Ravana faced each other. The skies echoed with rumbling thunders. Ravana deliberately took ten bows in ten of his hands and notched ten arrows to the bows. Rama reached for his bow also. Ravana let loose the arrows at Rama. Just as quickly, Rama shot each of the arrows out of the sky. Ravana's arrows now fell like showers of rain, thick as a hailstorm, they filled the sky and seemed to make a roof over Lanka. Still Rama managed to turn the arrows away.

Ravana was so angry that he jerked his chariot aside and ran through the monkey army, killing all who stood in his way. Rama could not stand by and see thousands of his soldiers die. He drove his chariot after Ravana. He chased Ravana off the battlefield and round all the skies of the world. Rama used his bow well, and arrow after arrow found Ravana's body.

The Last Battle

Ravana knew that ordinary weapons would not beat Rama. He thought that he would have to use his strangest and most powerful magic. He called up terrible spells and hurled them at Rama. One of the spells made all the dead soldiers of the demon army come to life again and begin to attack Rama. Rama was not frightened by the ghost demons. He called up the strength of his wisdom against the spell and the demons vanished.

Ravana worked another spell and more magic arrows appeared. These arrows were headed with terrible eyes and teeth and tongues of fire. They sped across the sky towards Rama carrying darkness and fear with them. Rama stayed calm and remembered the spell that would destroy such demon arrows.

Ravana next filled the air with snakes and dragons that made fiery poisons. Rama called up the holy eagles who could destroy them. Ravana came closer, firing showers of poison arrows at Rama. Rama turned the arrows back on Ravana. Rama and Ravana were very close together.

Rama drew his sword. With a mighty blow he cut off one of Ravana's heads. A new head grew in its place and the old head fell to the ground, swearing at Prince Rama. Rama swung again and this time he cut off two of Ravana's arms. New arms grew straight away, and the old arms tried to attack Rama as they fell squirming to the ground.

At last Rama remembered a specially holy power that had been used once by the Creator of the World on an evil monster. Rama called up this power with a prayer. He aimed the power full-force at Ravana's heart. Ravana had protected his head and his arms and body, but nothing guarded his evil heart. He was struck so hard that he fell from his chariot dead. The war was over.

59

Peace

Rama sent Hanuman to find Sita. She was so full of happiness she could hardly speak. She was free at last. Attendants waited on her and she was bathed and dressed and brought to Rama. The gods blessed Sita and offered to reward Rama for all that he had done. Rama asked the gods to give back life to all the monkeys and bears who had been killed in the war. Rama's request was granted and the monkeys and their friends were full of joy. So, peace came to the island of Lanka.

A great thanksgiving feast was held and Rama remembered that the fourteen years of his exile were almost over. Soon he would be able to return to the land of his father.

It was then time for the travellers to leave. The gods gave them a wonderful flying chariot and Rama, Sita and Lakshmana as well as Hanuman and all their new friends stepped into it, for the journey back, each to his own homeland. The chariot lifted them up into the air and they crossed the sea between Lanka and India. The friends looked down on the roads and paths that they had travelled years before. They passed over the forest where the three of them had once lived.

Eventually they came to Rama's own kingdom and to the palace where his father had once been king. Bharata was waiting for them. Twice times seven years had passed. Rama's time of exile was over.

61

The Kingdom of Rama

Bharata and Shatrughna were delighted to see Rama, Lakshmana and Sita. Bharata ordered the palace to be decorated and the whole city to be made splendid for Rama's coronation. The messengers went out once more bearing news of Rama's coronation, as they had done fourteen years earlier. The three mothers embraced their sons. Rama forgave Queen Kaikeyi the wrong she had done him so long ago.

Bharata told Rama that the country had been well ruled while he had been away in exile. The people were happy and there was food and wealth enough for all. Great crowds came to the palace to see Rama; and Rama and Sita prepared themselves for the coronation. The throne was decked out and Rama and Sita were clad in beautiful clothes. Then, at last, Rama was pronounced king in the land of his father, and Sita was crowned his queen.

Rama and Sita sat on their throne. Lakshmana stood closest to Rama, still fully devoted to the service of his beloved brother. At their feet knelt Hanuman, ever ready to spring into action to aid his friends.

The celebrations lasted for a whole month and every person who was present remembered the feasts and the joy that was shared by all.

And so began the reign of King Rama and Queen Sita —a time when peace and plenty filled the land, and happiness and holiness made earth, for a time, a little like heaven.